Get well
SIP1

An imprint of Om Books International

Reprinted in 2016

An imprint of Om Books International

Corporate & Editorial Office
A 12, Sector 64, Noida 201 301
Uttar Pradesh, India
Phone: +91 120 477 4100
Email: editorial@ombooks.com
Website: www.ombooksinternational.com

Sales Office
107, Ansari Road, Darya Ganj, New Delhi 110 002, India
Phone: +91 11 4000 9000
Fax: +91 11 2327 8091
Email: sales@ombooks.com
Website: www.ombooks.com

ISBN : 978-93-84119-55-3

Printed in India

10 9 8 7 6 5 4 3

Get well soon,
SIPPO

Paste your
photograph here

My name is

_____

Sippo the Hippo had not gone to school for two days. His friends Leapo the Leopard and Dina the Doe were worried. "Where is Sippo? Let's go and meet him," said Leapo.

Leapo rang the doorbell. Sippo's mother answered the door.

"Hello, Aunty. Is Sippo at home?" asked Dina.

"Yes, but he's ill. He's sleeping in his room," replied Sippo's mother, looking sad.

"What happened?" asked Dina.
"Last week, his uncle got chocolates, cakes and candies for Sippo! I told him not to eat all of them. But he ate them all and fell sick," replied his mother.

"We shall come to see him again," they said and left Sippo's house.
"Let's cheer Sippo up! He seems really unwell," said Dina.
"What can we do?" asked Leapo.

Leapo and Dina had an idea.
The next day, they met at Leapo's house
after school.

Leapo's mother helped them cook a
hot vegetable broth.

Dina put together a fruit basket.
It had apples, bananas, oranges and some
juicy pears. Then she tied a bow to the
basket. Now it was time to make the
cheer-up card!

Leapo got paper, paints and a pen. He folded the sheet neatly in half. Dina poured black paint in a bowl. Leapo made paw prints on one side of the card.

When the paint was dry, Dina added her paw prints on the other side of the card. She wrote a note for Sippo and put it in an envelope.

Leapo and Dina took the broth, fruit basket and card. They put them outside Sippo's door, rang the doorbell and hid behind a tree. Sippo's mother opened the door. She saw the card.

"Get well soon, Sippo!" said the card. "Look, Sippo! Someone left a surprise for you by the door," said Sippo's mother. She fed him the lovely broth. Sippo could not wait to see the card!

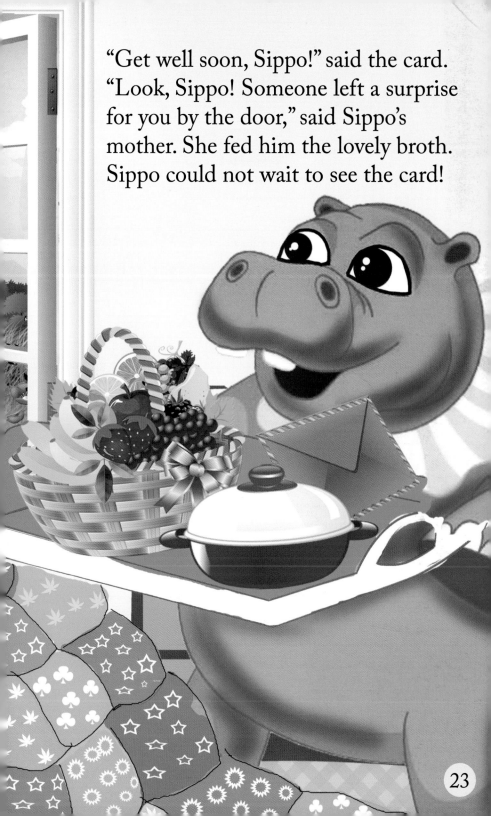

We miss the colou[r]
when you are gon[e]

Get well soo[n]
SIPPO!

24

Sippo saw the black paw prints
on the card. The card read:
"We miss the colour when
you are gone!
Get well soon, Sippo!"
Sippo got out of bed,
feeling better already.

Just then, he heard a knock on his window. But he saw no one.
He heard another knock. This time, he went to open the window.

He did not see anyone outside. "Where's that sound coming from?" Sippo thought to himself.

"Tadaaaaaaaa!" Leapo and Dina sprang up! They were hiding under the window to surprise Sippo.

Leapo and Dina got into the room from the window. The three friends hugged each other.